NUMBER 853

THE ENGLISH EXPERIENCE

ITS RECORD IN EARLY PRINTED BOOKS
PUBLISHED IN FACSIMILE

NICHOLAS BRETON

THE GOOD AND THE BADDE

LONDON, 1616

WALTER J. JOHNSON, INC.
THEATRUM ORBIS TERRARUM, LTD.
AMSTERDAM 1977 NORWOOD, N.J.

The publishers acknowledge their gratitude to
the Curators of the Bodleian Library, Oxford,
for their permission to reproduce the Library's
copy, Shelfmark: 4^0.B.52 Th.(1).

S.T.C. No. 3656

Collation: A-F^4.

Published in 1977 by

Theatrum Orbis Terrarum, Ltd.
Keizersgracht 526, Amsterdam

&

Walter J. Johnson, Inc.
355 Chestnut Street
Norwood, New Jersey
07648

Printed in the Netherlands

ISBN: 90 221 0853 8

Library of Congress Catalog Card Number
77-006859

THE GOOD

AND

THE BADDE,

OR

Descriptions of the

Worthies, and Vnworthies
of this Age.

WHERE
The Best may see their Graces, and
the worst discerne their Basenesse.

LONDON,
Printed by *George Purslowe* for *Iohn Budge*, and are to be
sold at the great South-dore of Paules,
and at *Brittaines Bursse*.
1616.

TO
THE RIGHT
VVORSHIPFVLL

and VVorthy, *Sir Gilbert Houghton,*
of Houghton *Knight*, *the Noble fauourer of all*
vertuous ſpirits : the higheſt power of hea-
uen grant the bleſsing of all happineſſe
to his worthy hearts deſire.

VVorthy Knight :

He worthineſſe of this ſub-
iect, in which is ſet downe,
the difference of light and
darkeneſſe, in the nature
of Honour and diſgrace,
to the deſeruers of either, hath made me
(vpon the note of the Nobleneſſe of
your ſpirit) like the Eagle, ſtill looking
towards the Sunne ; to preſent to your

A 3   patience,

DEDICATORY.

patience, the Patronage of this little
Treatise, of the Worthies and Vn-
worthies of this Age : *Wherein, I*
hope, you will finde some things to your
content, nothing to the contrary : which
leauing to the acceptance of your good
fauour, with my further seruice to your
command : J humbly rest,

Your Worships

deuoted, to be

commanded,

Nicholas Breton.

TO THE READER.

I Am sure that if you read thorough this Booke, you will finde your description in one place or other: if among the Worthies, holde you where you are, and change not your Carde for a worse: If among the other, mend that is amisse and all will be well. I name you not, for I know you not; but, I will wish the best, because the worst is too bad: I hope there will no body be angry, except it be, with himselfe for some-what that hee findes out of order, if it bee so, the hope is the greater, the bad will be no worse: yet the world being at such a passe, that liuing Creatures are scarcely knowne from pictures till they moue, nor Wise-men from fooles till they speake, nor Arteists from Bunglers, till they worke; I will onely wish the Worthy their worth, and the contrary, what may mend their Condition; and for my selfe but pardon for my presumption,

tion , in writing vpon the natures of more
worth then I am worthy to write of , and fa-
uourable acceptation of no worthy intention of reprehenſion , by the leaſt thought of
malicious diſpoſition.   So leauing my booke
to your beſt like , with my better labours to
the like effect : In hope to finde you among
the Worthies : I reſt,

At your command, if worthy, N. B.

THE GOOD

AND

THE BADDE:

OR,

Descriptions of the Worthies, and Vnworthies of this Age.

A Worthy KING.

Worthy King is a figure of God, in the nature of gouernment: he is the chiefe of men, and the Churches Champion, Natures honour, and Earths maiesty: is the director of Law, and the strength of the same, the Sword of Iustice and the Scepter of Mercy, the Glasse of Grace, and the Eye of Honour, the Terror of Treason, and the Life of Loyalty. His commaund is general, and his power absolute, his frowne a death, and his fauour a life, his charge is his subiects, his care their safety, his pleasure their peace, and his ioy their loue: he is not to be paraleld, because he is without equalitie, and the prerogatiue of his Crowne must not be contradicted: hee is the Lords Anointed, and therfore must not be touched, and the Head of a publique body, and therfore must

B

bee

be preferued : he is a fcourge of finne, and a bleffing
of Grace, Gods Vicegerent ouer his people, and
vnder him fupreme Gouernour, his fafety muft bee
his Councels care, his health, his Subiects prayer,
his pleafure, his Peeres comfort; and his content, his
Kingdomes gladneffe : his prefence muft be reue-
renced, his Perfon attended, his Court adorned, and
his State maintained ; his bofome muft not be fear-
ched, his will not difobeyed, his wants not vnfuppli-
ed, nor his place vnregarded. In fumme, he is more
then a man, though not a God, and next vnder God
to be honoured aboue man.

An Vnworthy King.

2   AN Vnworthy King, is the vfurper of Power,
where tyranny in authority lofeth the glory
of maiefty, while the feare of terror frighteth loue from obedience: For when the Lyon plaies
the Wolfe, the Lambe dies with the Ewe. Hee is a
meffenger of Worth to be the fcourge of finne, or
the triall of patience, in the hearts of the religious :
he is a warrant of woe, in the execution of his fury,
and in his beft temper, a doubt of Grace : hee is a
difpeopler of his Kingdome, and a prey to his ene-
mies, an vndelightfull friend, and a tormentor of
himfelfe : he knowes no God, but makes an Idoll of
Nature, and vfeth Reafon but to the ruine of fenfe :
his care is but his will, his pleafure but his eafe, his
exercife but finne ; and his delight but vnhumane :
his heauen is his pleafure, and his golde is his God :
his prefence is terrible, his countenance horrible, his
words

words vncomfortable, and his actions intolerable. In summe, he is the foyle of a Crowne, the disgrace of a Court, the trouble of a Councell, and the plague of a Kingdome.

A Worthy Queene.

A Worthy Queene is the figure of a King, who vnder God in his Grace, hath a great power ouer his people: She is the chiefe of women, the beauty of her Court, and the grace of her Sexe in the royalty of her spirit: She is like the moone, that giueth light among the starres, and but vnto the Sunne, giues none place in her brightnesse: She is the pure Diamond vpon the Kings finger, and the Orient Pearle vnprizeable in his eye, the ioy of the Court in the comfort of the King, and the wealth of the kingdome in the fruit of her loue: Shee is Reasons honour, in Natures grace, and Wisedomes loue in Vertues beautie. In summe, she is the Handmaid of God, and the Kings second selfe, and in his Grace, the beauty of a Kingdome.

3

A Worthy Prince.

A Worthy Prince is the hope of a kingdom, the richest Iewell in a Kings Crowne, and the fairest flowre in the Queenes garden: hee is the ioy of Nature in the hope of Honour, and the loue of Wisedome, in the life of Worthinesse: In the secret carriage of his hearts intention, til his dissignes come to action, he is a dumbe shew to the Worlds

4

ima-

imagination: in his wifedome hee ftartles the fpirits of expectation in his valour, he fubiects the hearts of Ambition in his Vertue, hee winnes the loue of the Nobleft, and in his bounty bindes the feruice of the moft fufficient : he is the Cryftall glaffe , where Nature may fee her comfort; and the booke of Reafon, where Vertue may reade her honour : Hee is the Morning-ftarre, that hath light from the Sunne, and the bleffed fruit of the Tree of Earths Paradife : hee is the ftudie of the wife in the ftate of Honour , and in the fubiect of Learning, the hiftory of admiration. In fumme, he is in the note of wifdome, the aime of Honour, and in the honour of Vertue the hope of a Kingdome.

An Vnworthy Prince.

5   AN Vnworthy Prince is the feare of a kingdome, when will and power carrie Pride in impatience, in the clofe cariage of ambitious intention, he is like a fearefull dreame to a troubled fpirit : in his paffionate humours he frighteth the hearts of the prudent, in the delight of vanities hee lofeth the loue of the wife , and in the mifery of Auarice is ferued onely with the needy : he is like a little mift, before the rifing of the Sunne, which, the more it growes, the leffe good it doth : Hee is the Kings griefe , and the Queenes forrowe, the Courts trouble, and the Kingdomes curfe. In fumme, he is the feede of vnhappineffe, the fruit of vngodlineffe, the tafte of bitterneffe , and the digeftion of heauineffe.

A Worthie Priuie Counceller.

AWorthy Priuie Counceller is the Pillar of a
Realme, in whofe wifedome and care, vnder
GOD, and the King, ftands the fafety of a
Kingdome : He is the Watch-towre to giue war-
ning of the Enemy, and a hand of prouifion for the
preferuation of the State : hee is an Oracle in the
Kings eare, and a Sword in the Kings hand, an euen
weight in the ballance of Iuftice, and a light of grace
in the loue of truth : he is an eye of care in the courfe
of lawe, a heart of loue in his feruice to his Soueraigne, a mind of honour in the order of his feruice,
and a braine of inuention for the good of the Common-wealth : his place is powerfull, while his feruice is faithfull, and his honour due in the defert of
his employment. In fumme, hee is as a fixed Planet
mong the ftarres of the Firmament, which through
the Cloudes in the ayre, fhewes the nature of his
light.

6

An Vnworthie Counceller.

AN vnworthy Counceller is the hurt of a King,
and the danger of a State, when the weaknes
of iudgement may commit an error, or the
lacke of care may giue way to vnhappineffe : he is a
wicked charme in the Kings eare, a fword of terror
in the aduice of tyranny : His power is per llous in
the partiality of will, and his heart full of hollow-
neffe in the proteftation of loue : Hypocrifie is the

7

couer

couer of his counterfaite religion, and traiterous in-
uḗtion is the Agent of his Ambition:He is the cloud
of darkeneſſe, that threatneth foule weather; and if
it growe to a ſtorme, it is fearefull where it falls : hee
is an enemy to God in the hate of Grace, and worthie of death in diſloyalty to his Soueraigne. In
ſumme,he is an vnfit perſon for the place of a Counceller, and an vnworthy Subieᵭt to looke a King in
the face.

A Noble man.

8

ANoble man is a marke of Honour, where
the eye of wiſedome in the obſeruation of deſert ſees the fruit of Grace: hee is the Orient
Pearle that Reaſon poliſheth for the beauty of Nature, and the Diamond ſparke where diuine Grace
giues Vertue honour : he is the Note-booke of Morall Diſcipline, where the conceit of care may finde
the true Courtier : he is the Nurſe of hoſpitality, the
reliefe of neceſſitie, the loue of Charity, and the life
of Bounty : hee is Learnings grace, and Valours
fame, Wiſedomes fruit, and kindneſſe loue : hee is
the true Falcon that feedes on no Carrion, the true
Horſe that will bee no Hackney, the true Dolphin
that feares not the Whale,and the true man of God,
that feares not the diuell.   In ſumme, he is the Darling of Nature, in Reaſons Philoſophy ; the Load-
ſtarre of light in Loues Aſtronomie, the rauiſhing
Sweet in the muſique of Honour, and the golden
number in Graces Arithmeticke.

An

An Vnnoble man.

AN Vnnoble man is the griefe of Reaſo, when the title of Honour is put vpon the ſub-iect of diſgrace; when, either the imperfe-ction of wit, or the folly of will ſhewes an vnfitneſſe in Nature for the vertue of Aduancement : he is the eye of baſeneſſe, and ſpirit of groſſeneſſe, and in the demeane of rudeneſſe the skorne of Nobleneſſe: he is a ſuſpicion of a right Generation in the nature of his diſpoſition, and a miſerable plague to a femi-nine patience : Wiſedome knowes him not, lear-ning bred him not, Vertue loues him not, and Ho-nour fits him not : Prodigality or Auarice are the notes of his inclination, and folly or miſchiefe are the fruits of his inuention. In ſumme, he is the ſhame of his name, the diſgrace of his place, the blot of his Title, and the ruine of his houſe.

9

A worthie Biſhop.

AWorthy Biſhop is an Ambaſſadour from God vnto man, in the midſt of warre to make a Treaty of peace; who, with a generall par-don vpon confeſſion of ſinne, vpon the fruit of Re-pentance, giues aſſurance of comfort : Hee brings tidings from heauen, of happineſſe to the World, where the patience of mercie calls Nature to Grace: Hee is the ſiluer Trumpet in the muſicke of Loue, where faith hath a life that neuer failes the beloued : Hee is the Director of life in the Lawes of God, and the

10

the Chirurgion of the Soule, in launcing the fores
of finne, the terror of the Reprobate, in pronoun-
cing their damnation ; and the ioy of the faithfull,
in the affurance of their faluation.   In fumme, hee
is in the nature of Grace, worthy of Honour, and in
the meffage of Life, worthy of Loue : a continuall
Agent betwixt God and man, in the preaching of
his Word, and Prayer for his people.

An Vnworthy Bifhop.

11   A N Vnworthy Bifhop is the difgrace of Lear-
ning, when the want of reading, or the abufe
of vnderftanding, in the fpeech of Error
may beget Idolatry. He is Gods enemy, in the hurt
of his people, and his owne woe, in abufe of the
Word of God : he is the fhadow of a Candle, that
giues no light ; or, if it be any, it is but to leade into
darkeneffe : the Sheepe are vnhappy, that liue in
his fold, when they fhall either ftarue, or feede on
ill ground : hee breeds a warre in the wits of his Au-
dience, when his life is contrary to the nature of his
inftruction : hee liues in a roome, where he troubles
a World, and in the fhadow of a Saint, is little better then a Deuill ; hee makes Religion a cloake of
finne, and with counterfeit Humility, couereth in-
comparable Pride. Hee robs the rich, to relieue
the poore, and makes fooles of the wife, with the i-
magination of his worth : hee is all for the Church,
but, nothing for God, and for the eafe of Nature, lofeth the ioy of Reafon.   In fumme, he is the picture
of Hypocrifie, the fpirit of Herefie ; a wound in the
Church,

Church, and a woe in the World.

A worthy Iudge.

A Iudge is a Doome, whofe breath is mortall vpon the breach of Law, where Criminall offences muft bee cut off from a commonwealth: Hee is a fword of Iuftice in the hand of a King; and, an Eye of Wifedome in the walke of a kingdome: his ftudy is a Square for the keeping of proportion, betwixt command, and obedience, that the King may keepe his Crowne on his head, and the Subie&t his head on his fhoulders. Hee is feared but of the foolifh, and curfed but of the wicked; but, of the wife honoured, and of the gracious beloued : Hee is a furueier of rights, and reuenger of wrongs, and in the iudgement of Truth, the Honor of Iuftice. In fumme, his word is Law, his power Grace, his labour Peace, and his defert Honour.

12

An vnworthy Iudge.

A N vnworthy Iudge is the griefe of Iuftice in the Error of Iudgement, when, through ignorance, or will, the death of Innocency lies vpon the breath of Opinion : Hee is the difgrace of Law, in the defert of Knowledge, and the plague of Power, in the mifery of Oppreffion : He is more Morall, then Diuine, in the nature of Policy, and more Iudicious, then Iuft, in the carriage of his conceit : His Charity is cold, when partiality is refolued, when the doome of life lies on the

13

C

verdi&t

verdict of a Iury, with a ſterne looke, hee frighteth
an offender, and giues little comfort to a poore
mans cauſe. The golden weight ouerwaies his
Grace ; when Angels play the Diuels in the hearts
of his people. In ſumme, where Chriſt is prea-
ched, hee hath no place in his Church ; and in this
Kingdome, out of doubt, God will not ſuffer any
ſuch Diuell to beare ſway.

A Worthie Knight.

14   A Worthy Knight is a ſpirit of proofe, in the
aduancement of Vertue, by the deſert of
Honour, in the Eye of Maieſtie: In the field
hee giues courage to his Souldiers, in the Court,
Grace to his followers, in the Cittie, reputation to
his perſon, and in the Country honour to his Houſe.
His Sword and his Horſe make his way to his
Houſe, and his Armor of beſt proofe is an vndaunted Spirit; the Muſicke of his delight, is the Trumpet and the Drumme, and the Paradiſe of his Eye,
is an Army defeated, the reliefe of the oppreſſed,
makes his Conqueſt honourable, and the pardon of
the ſubmiſſiue makes him famous in mercy : Hee
is in Nature milde, and in Spirit ſtout, in Reaſon iudicious, and in all, Honourable. In ſumme, hee
is a Yeomans commander, & a Gentlemans ſuperi-
our, a Noble mans companion, and a Princes worthy fauourite.

An Vnworthy Knight.

AN Vnworthy Knight is the defect of Nature, in the title of Honour, when to maintaine Valor, his Spurres haue no rowels, nor his Sword a point; his apparell is of proofe, that may weare like his Armour, or like an olde Enſigne, that hath his honour in ragges. It may be he is the Taylors trouble in fitting an ill ſhape, or a Mercers wonder, in wearing of Silke; in the Court he ſtands for a Cipher, and among Ladies like an Owle among Birds: Hee is worſhipt onely for his wealth, and if hee be of the firſt head, hee ſhall be valued by his wit, when if his pride goe beyond his purſe, his Title will be a trouble to him. In ſumme, hee is the Child of Folly, and the man of Gotham, the blind man of Pride, and the foole of imagination: But in the Court of Honour, are no ſuch Apes, and I hope that this Kingdome will breed no ſuch Aſſes.

15

A Worthy Gentleman.

A Worthy Gentleman, is a branch of the tree of Honour, whoſe fruites are the actions of Vertue, as pleaſing to the Eye of Iudgement, as taſtefull to the Spirit of vnderſtanding: whatſoeuer hee doth, it is not forced, except it bee euill, which either through ignorance vnwittingly; or, through compulſion vnwillingly, he fals vpon, hee in Nature kinde, in Demeanour courteous, in Alleageance loyall, and in Religion zealous, in ſeruice

16

C 2 faithfull,

faithfull, and in reward Bountifull : Hee is made
of no Baggage stuffe, nor, for the wearing of base
people ; but is wouen by the Spirit of Wisedome,
to adorne the Court of Honour. His apparell is
more comely then costly , and his Diet more whol-
some then excessiue, his Exercise more healthfull
then painefull, and his Study more for Knowledge
then Pride ; his Loue not wanton, nor common,
his gifts not niggardly, nor prodigall : and his carriage neither Apish, nor sullen. In summe, he is an
approuer of his Pedigree, by the Noblenesse of his
passage, and, in the course of his life, an example to
his posterity.

An Vnworthy Gentleman.

17 AN Vnworthy Gentleman is the scoffe of
Wit, and the scorne of Honour, where more
wealth then wit is worshipt of Simplicity :
who spends more in Idlenesse , then would maintaine Thrift, or hides more in Misery, then might
purchase Honour : whose delights are Vanities,
and whose pleasures Fopperies, whose studies Fables, and, whose exercise, worse then Follies : His
conuersation is Base, and his conference Ridiculous,
his affections Vngracious, and his actions Ignomi-
nious.   His Apparell out of fashion, and his Diet
out of order, his Cariage out of square , and, his
company out of request. In summe, he is like a mun-
grell Dogge with a veluet Coller, a Cart-Horse
with a golden Saddle, a Buzzard kite with a Fawl-
cons Bels, or a Baboune with a pied Ierkin.

A Worthy Lawyer.

A Worthy Lawyer is the Studient of know-ledge, how to bring controuersies into a con-clusion of Peace, and out of ignorance to gaine vnderstanding : Hee diuides Time into vses, and Cases into conftructions : Hee layes open ob-scurities, and is prayfed for the speech of Truth, and in the Court of Confcience pleads much in *Forma pauperis*, for finall fees : He is a meane for the pre-feruation of Titles, and the holding of poffeffi-ons, and a great inftrument of Peace in the Iudge-ment of impartiality : Hee is the Clyents hope, in his Cafes pleading, and his hearts comfort in a happy iffue : Hee is the finder out of Tricks in the craft of ill confcience, and the ioy of the diftref-fed in the reliefe of Iuftice. In fumme, hee is a maker of Peace, among the Spirits of Contention, & a continuer of quiet, in the execution of the Law.

18

An Vnworthy Lawyer.

AN Vnlearned and vnworthily called a Lawy-er, is the figure of a Foot-poft, who carries Letters, but knowes not what is in them, only can read the fuperfcriptions, to direct them to their right owners. So trudgeth this fimple Clarke, that can fcarce read a Cafe when it is written, with his hand-full of papers, from one Court to another, and from one Counfellors chamber to another, when by his good payment, for his paines, hee will bee fo fawcy, as to call himfelfe a Sollicitor :

19

But

But what a taking are poore Clients in, when this too much trusted cunning companion, better read in *Pierce Plowman*, then in *Ploydon*, and in the Play of *Richard* the Third, then in the Pleas of *Edward* the Fourth; perswades them all is sure, when hee is sure of all ? and in what a misery are the poore men, when, vpon a *Nihil dicit*, because indeede, this poore fellow, *Nihil potest dicere*, they are in danger of an Execution, before they know wherefore they are condemned : But, I wish all such more wicked then witty, vnlearned in the Law and abusers of the same, to looke a little better into their consciences, and to leaue their crafty courses, lest when the Law indeede laies them open, in steade of carrying papers in their hands, they weare not papers on their heads, and in stead of giuing eare to their Clients causes, or rather eies into their purses, they haue nere an Eare left to heare withal, nor good Eie to see withall; or at least honest Face to looke out withall : but as the Grashoppers of Egypt, bee counted the Caterpillers of England, and not the Foxe that stole the Goose, but the great Foxe that stole the Farme, from the Gander.

A Worthy Souldier.

20

A Worthy Souldier is the childe of Valour, who was borne for the seruice of necessitie, and to beare the Ensigne of Honour, in the actions of Worth : He is the Dyer of the Earth with blood, and the ruine of the erections of Pride: Hee is the watch of Wit, in the aduantage of Time,

and

and the executioner of Wrath vpon the wilfull offender : He diſputes queſtions with the point of a Sword, and preferres Death to indignities : Hee is a Lyon to Ambition, and a Lambe to Submiſſion: hee hath Hope faſt by the hand, and treads vpon the head of Feare.   Hee is the Kings Champion, and the Kingdomes Guard, Peaces preſeruer , and Rebellions terror : He makes the Horſe trample at the ſound of a Trumpet, and leades on to a battaile, as if hee were going to a break-faſt; hee knowes not the nature of Cowardiſe, for his reſt is ſet vp vpon Reſolution : his ſtrongeſt fortification is his Mind, which beates off the aſſaults of idle humors, and his life is the paſſage of danger, where, an vndaunted Spirit ſtoopes to no Fortune; with his armes hee wins his Armes, and by his deſert in the field, his Honour in the Court.   In ſumme, in the trueſt Man-hood hee is the true man : and in the creation of Honour , a moſt worthy Creature.

An Vntrained Souldier.

AN Vntrained Souldier is like a young hound, that when the firſt falls to hunt, he knowes not how to lay his noſe to the earth: Who hauing his name but in a booke, and marched twiſe about a market place, when he comes to a piece of ſeruice, knowes not how to beſtowe himſelfe : He marches as if he were at plough , carries his Pike like a Pike-ſtaffe, and his ſword before him , for feare of loſing from his ſide : if he be a Shot, he will be rather ready to ſay a Grace ouer his Peece, and ſo to diſcharge his

21

his hands of it , then to learne how to difcharge it
with a grace : he puts on his Armour ouer his eares,
like a wafte-coate, and weares his Murrian like a
night-cap ; when he is quartered in the field, he looks
for his bed, and when he fees his Prouant , he is rea-
die to crie for his victuals ; and ere hee knowe well
where he is, wifh heartily hee were at home againe,
with hanging downe his head, as if his heart were in
his hofe : fleepe till a Drumme , or a deadly bullet
awake him , and fo carrie himfelfe in all Companies,
that till Martiall Difcipline haue feafoned his vnderftanding, he is like a Cipher among figures, an Owle
among birds, a Wife man among fooles, and a fhadow among men.

A Worthy Phyfician.

22   A Worthy Phyfician is the enemy of ficknefle,
in purging nature from corruption : his action is moft in feeling of pulfes , and his difcourfes chiefely of the natures of difeafes : He is a
great fearcher out of fimples , and accordingly
makes his compofition : hee perfwades abftinence,
and patience, for the benefit of health, while purge-
ing and bleeding are the chiefe courfes of his counfaile : the Apothecarie, and the Chirurgeon are his
two chiefe attendants , with whom conferring vpon
Time, growes temperate in his cures : Surfets, and
wantonneffe are great agents for his imploiment,
when by the fecret of his skill, out of others weaknes
hee gathers his owne ftrength. In fumme, hee is a
                                                        necef-

neceſſary member for an vnneceſſary malady, to find
a diſeaſe and to cure the diſeaſed.

An Vnworthy Phyſician.

AN vnlearned, and ſo Vnworthy Phyſician, is
a kinde of Horſe-leech, whoſe cure is moſt in
drawing of bloud, and a deſperate purge, either to cure, or kill, as it hits; his diſcourſe is moſt
of the cures that hee hath done, and them afarre off:
and not a receipt vnder a hundreth pounds, though
it be not worth three halfe-pence : Vpon the market day he is much haunted with Vrinals, where if he
finde any thing (though he knowe nothing) yet hee
will ſay ſome-what, which if it hit to ſome purpoſe,
with a fewe fuſtian words, hee will ſeeme a piece of
ſtrange ſtuffe : hee is neuer without old merry tales,
and ſtale Ieſts to make olde folkes laugh, and Cum-
fits, or Plummes in his pocket, to pleaſe little Children : yea, and he will be talking of complexions,
though he know nothing of their diſpoſitions : and if
his medicine doe a feate, he is a made man among
fooles : but being wholly vnlearned, and oft-times
vnhoneſt, let me thus briefly deſcribe him : He is a
plaine kinde of Mountebanke, and a true *Quacke-*
ſaluer, a danger for the ſicke to deale withall, and a
Dizard in the world to talke withall.

23

D

A worthy Marchant.

24

A Worthy Marchant is the heire of aduenture, whofe hopes hang much vpon winde : Vpon a wodden horfe he rides through the world, and in a merry Gale, makes a path through the Seas: he is a difcouerer of Countries, and a finder out of commodities, refolute in his attempts, and royall in his expences : he is the life of Traffick, and the maintainer of Trade, the Sailers Mafter, and the Souldiers friend ; hee is the exercife of the exchange, the honor of credit, the obferuation of Time, and the vnderftanding of thrift : his ftudie is number, his care his accounts, his comfort his Confcience, and his wealth his good Name : he feares not *Silla*, and fayles clofe by *Caribdis*, and hauing beaten out a ftorme, rides at reft in a harbour: by his Sea gaine, he makes his land-purchafe, and by the knowledge of Trade, findes the key of Treafure : out of his trauailes, he makes his difcourfes, and from his eye-obferuations, brings the Moddels of Architectures ; he plants the earth with forraine fruits, and knowes at home what is good abroad : he is neat in apparell, modeft in demeanure, dainty in dyet, and ciuill in his carriage. In fumme, hee is the Pillar of a City, the enricher of a Country, the furnifher of a Court, and the worthy feruant of a King.

An

An Vnworthy Marchant.

A N Vnworthy Merchant is a kinde of Pedler, who (with the helpe of a Broker) gets more by his wit, then by his honeftie : hee doth fometime vfe to giue out money to Gamefters, bee paide in poft, vpon a hand at Dice : fometime, he gaines more by Bawbles, then better Stuffes, and rather then faile, wil aduenture a falfe oath for a fraudulent gaine; hee deales with no whole fale, but all his honefty is at one word: as for wares and weights he knows how to hold the ballance, and for his Confcience, he is not ignorant what to do with it: his trauaile is moft by land, for he fears to be too bufie with the water , and whatfoeuer his ware be, hee will be fure of his money : the moft of his wealth is in a packe of trifles, and for his honefty, I dare not paffe my word for him ; if he be rich, tis tenne to one of his pride, and if he be poore, he breakes without his faft. In fumme , hee is the difgrace of a Marchant, the difhonour of a Citty , the difcredit of his parifh, and the diflike of all.

25

A good man.

A Good man is an image of God, Lord ouer all his Creatures, and created only for his feruice : he is made capable of Reafon, to know the properties of Nature, and by the infpiration of Grace, to know things fupernaturall : He hath a face

26

alwaies to looke vpward , and a Soule that giues life
to all the Sences, hee liues in the VVorld as a Stran-
ger, while Heauen is the home of his fpirit : his life
is but the labour of fence ; and his death , the way
to his reft : his ftudy is the word of fruth , and his
delight is in the lawe of loue : his prouifion is but to
ferue neceffity, and his care the exercife of Charitie:
he is more conuerfant with the diuine Prophets,then
the worlds profits , and makes the ioy of his foule in
the tidings of his faluation: he is wife in the beft wit,
and wealthy in the richeft treafure : his hope is but
the comfort of mercy , and his feare but the hurt of
finne : Pride is the hate of his foule, and Patience
the worker of his peace , his Guide is the wifedome
of Grace, and his trauaile but to the heauenly *Ieru-
falem.* In fumme, hee is the Elect of God, the bleffing of Grace , the feede of loue , and the fruite of
life.

An Atheift, or moft badde man.

27   AN Atheift is a figure of defperation , who
dare do any thing euen to his foules damnation : he is in nature a Dogge, in wit an Affe,
in paffion a Bedlam , and in action a Diuell : Hee
makes Sinne a ieft, Grace an humour, Truth a fable,
and Peace a Cowardice : his Horfe is his pride, his
Sword is his Caftle, his Apparell his riches , and
his Punke his Paradife : hee makes Robberie his
purchafe , Lechery his Solace , Mirth his Exercife , and Drunkenneffe his Glory ; hee is the
danger

daunger of Society , the loue of Vanitie, the hate
of Charitie , and the fhame of Humanitie : hee is
Gods enemie, his Parents griefe , his Countries
plague, and his owne confufion; hee fpoiles that is
necefsarie, and fpends that is needlefse; he fpightes
at the Gracious, and fpurnes at the Godly : the Ta-
uerne is his Palace, & his belly is his God, a VVhore
is his Miftris, and the Diuell is his Mafter : Oathes
are his Graces, VVounds his Badges; Shifts are his
practices, and beggery his paiments : Hee knowes
not G O D , nor thinkes of Heauen , but walkes
thorow the world, as a Diuell towards Hell : Vertue
knowes him not , Honefty findes him not, VVife-
dome loues him not, and Honour regards him not:
hee is but the Cutlers friend, and the Chirurgeons
Agent, the Thiefes Companion, and the Hang-
mans Benefactor : he was begotten vntimely, and
borne vnhappily, liues vngracioufly,and dies vnchri-
ftianly : Hee is of no Religion, nor good fafhion,
hardly good complexion , & moft vile in condition.
In fumme , hee is a Monfter among men, a Iewe a-
mong Chriftians , a foole among VVifemen, and a
diuell among Saints.

A wife

A Wise man.

28

A Wise man, is a Clocke that neuer ſtrikes but at his houre, or rather like a Diall, that being ſet right with the Sunne, keepes his true courſe in his compaſſe. So the heart of a Wiſe man, ſet in the courſe of Vertue by the ſpirit of Grace, runnes the courſe of life, in the compaſſe of eternall comfort : Hee meaſureth Time, and tempreth Nature, imployeth Reaſon, and commandeth Senſe : Hee hath a deafe Eare to the Charmer, a cloſe mouth to the Slaunderer, an open hand to Charity, and an humble mind to Piety : Obſeruation and experience are his reaſons labours, and Patience with Conſcience are the lines of his Loues meaſure, Contemplation, and Meditation are his Spirits exerciſe, and G O D and his Word are the ioy of his Soule : Hee knowes not the Pride of Proſperity, nor the miſery of Aduerſitie, but takes the one as the Day, the other as the Night : Hee knowes no Fortune, but builds all vpon prouidence, and through the hope of Faith, hath a fayre ayme at Heauen : His words are weighed with Iudgement, and, his Actions are the examples of Honour : Hee is fit for the ſeat of Authority, and deſerues the reuerence of Subiection : Hee is precious in the counſell of a King, and mighty in the ſway of a Kingdome. In ſumme, hee is Gods ſeruant, and the Worlds Maſter, a ſtranger vpon Earth, and a Citizen in Heauen.

A

A Foole.

A Foole is the Abortiue of wit, where Nature had more power then Reafon, in bringing forth the fruit of imperfection , his actions are moft in extremes, and the fcope of his braine is but Ignorance : onely Nature hath taught him to feede, and Vfe, to labour without knowledge : Hee is a kind of fhadow of a better fubftance, or, like the Vifion of a Dreame, that yeelds nothing awake : be is commonly knowne by one of two fpeciall Names, deriued from their qualities, as, from wilfull Will-foole,and Hodge from Hodge-podge; all meates are alike, all are one to a Foole : His exercifes are commonly diuided into foure parts , Eating and Drinking, Sleeping and Laughing: foure things are his chiefe Loues : a Bawble , and a Bell, a Coxe-combe, and a Pide-coate : Hee was begotten in vn-happineffe,borne to no goodnes, liues but in beaftli-neffe, and dies but in forgetfulneffe. In fumme, he is the fhame of Nature , the trouble of Wit, the charge of Charity, and the loffe of Liberality.

29

An Honeft man.

AN Honeft man is like a plaine Coate,which, without welt or gard, keepeth the body from winde and weather, and being well made, fits him beft that weares it; and where the ftuffe is more regarded then the fafhion, there is not much adoe in the putting of it on:fo,the mind of an Honeft man
without

30

without tricks or complements, keepes the credit of
a good Confcience from the fcandal of the World,
and the worme of Iniquity : which, being wrought,
by the Worke-man of Heauen , fits him beft that
weares it to his feruice : and, where Vertue is more
efteemed then Vanity, it is put on, and worne with
that eafe, that fhewes the excellency of the Worke-
man : His ftudy is Vertue , his word Truth, his life
the paffage of Patience, and his death the reft of his
Spirit : His trauaile is a Pilgrimage,his way is plain-
neffe, his pleafure Peace , and his delight is Loue :
His care is his Confcience, his wealth is his credit,
his charge is his Charity , and his content is his
Kingdome. In fumme, hee is a Diamond among
Iewels, a Phænix among Birds, an Vnicorne among
Beafts, and a Saint among men.

A Knaue.

AKnaue is the fcumme of Wit,and the fcorne
of Reafon, the hate of Wifedome , and the
difhonour of Humanity : He is the danger
of Society,and the hurt of Amity, the infection of
Youth,and the corruption of Age:He is a Traytor to
Affiance, and abufe to imployment, and a rule of
Villany, in a plot of mifchiefe : Hee hath a Cats
eye, and a Beares paw, a Sirens tongue, and a Ser-
pents fting : His Words are lies, his Oaths periu-
ries , his Studies fubtilties, and his practices Villa-
nies, his Wealth is his wit,his Honour is his wealth,
his Glory is his gaine, and his god is his Gold : He
is no mans friend, and his owne enemy, curfed on
Earth,

31

Earth, and banished from Heauen : Hee was begotten vngraciously, borne vntimely, liues disho-
nestly, and dies shamefully : His heart is a puddle
of Poyson, his Tongue a sting of iniquity, his Braine
a distiller of deceit, and his Conscience a compasse
of Hell. In summe, hee is a Dogge in disposition,
a Foxe in wit, a Wolfe in his prey , and a Diuell in
his Pride.

An Vsurer.

AN Vsurer is a figure of Misery , who hath
made himselfe a slaue to his Money : His
Eye is clos'd from pitty , and his hand from
Charity, his Eare from compassion , and his heart
from Piety : while hee liues, hee is the hate
of a Christian, and , when he dies , hee goes with
horror to hell : His study is sparing, and his care
is getting, his feare is wanting, and his death is loo-
sing : His Diet is either fasting, or poore fare , his
Cloathing the Hang-mans wardrobe, his house the
receptacle of Theeuery, and his Musick the chinking
of his Money : Hee is a kind of Canker, that with
the teeth of Interest, eates the hearts of the poore,
and a venimous Fly , that sucks out the blood of a-
ny flesh that hee lights on. In summe, hee is a ser-
uant of drosse, a slaue to Misery, an Agent for Hell,
and a Diuell in the World.

E

A Beggar.

33

A Beggar is the childe of Idlenesse, whose life is a resolution of ease, his trauaile is most in the High-wayes, and his *Randevows* is commonly in an Ale-house : His study is to counterfeit Impotency, and his practice, to cozen simplicity of Charity, the iuice of the Malt is the licour of his life, and at bed, and at boord a Louse is his companion : Hee feares no such enemy, as a Constable, and, beeing acquainted with the stocks, must visite them, as hee goes by them : Hee is a Drone that feedes vpon the labours of the Bee, and vnhappily begotten, that is borne for no goodnesse; his staffe and his scrippe are his walking furniture, and what hee lackes in meat, hee will haue out in drinke : He is a kinde of Caterpiller that spoiles much good fruite, and an vnprofitable creature to liue in a common-wealth : Hee is seldome handsome, and often noysome, alwaies troublesome, and neuer welcome: hee prayes for all, and preyes vpon all, begins with blessing, but ends often with cursing : if hee haue a Licence, hee shewes it with a grace, but if hee haue none, hee is submissiue to the ground : sometime he is a Thiefe, but, alwaies a Rogue, and in the nature of his profession, the shame of Humanity. In sum, hee is commonly begot in a Bush, borne in a Barne, liues in a High-way, and dyes in a Ditch.

A

A *Virgin.*

A Virgin is the beauty of Nature, where the
Spirit gracious makes the creature Glorious:
She is the loue of Vertue, the honour of Reason, the grace of Youth, and the comfort of Age :
Her studie is Holinesse, her exercise Goodnesse, her
grace Humility, and her loue is Charity : her countenance is Modesty; her speech is Truth, her wealth
Grace, and her fame Constancy : her vertue Conti-
nence, her labour Patience, her dyet Abstinence,
and her care Conscience : Her conuersation Heauenly, her meditations Angel-like, her prayers De-
uout, and her hopes Diuine : Her parents Ioy,
her kindreds Honour, her countreys Fame, and her
owne Felicity : She is the blessed of the Highest,
the praise of the Worthiest, the loue of the Noblest,
and the neerest to the Best : Shee is of creatures
the Rarest, of Women the Chiefest, of nature the
Purest, and of Wisedome the Choysest. Her life
is a Pilgrimage, her death but a Passage, her description a Wonder, and her name an Honour. In
summe, shee is the daughter of Glory, the mother
of Grace, the sister of Loue, and the beloued of
Life.

34

A *wanton Woman.*

A Wanton Woman is the figure of Imperfection, in nature, an Ape, in quality, a Wag-
taile, in countenance, a Witch, and in condition,

35

dition, a kinde of Diuell : her beck is a net,her word
a charme, her looke an illusion, and her companie a
confusion : her life is the play of idlenesse , her diet
the excesse of dainties, her loue the change of vanities , and her exercise the inuention of follies : her
pleasures are fansies, her studies fashions,her delight
colours, and her wealth her cloathes : her care is to
deceiue, her comfort her Company, her house is vanity, and her Bed is ruine , her discourses are fables,
her vowes,dissimulations,her conceits subtilties,and
her contents varieties : She would she knowes not
what, and spends she cares not what, she spoiles she
sees not what, and doth shee thinks not what : She
is Youths plague,and Ages Purgatory,Times abuse,
and Reasons trouble. In summe , shee is a spice of
madnesse, a sparke of mischiefe, a tutch of poyson,
and a feare of destruction.

A quiet Woman.

36

AQuiet woman is like a still winde , which neither chils the body , nor blowes dust in the
face: her Patience is a Vertue that winnes the
heart of loue, and her wisedome makes her will well
worthy regarde : She feares God, and flyeth sinne,
sheweth kindnesse and loueth peace: her tongue is ti-
ed to discretion, and her heart is the harbor of goodnesse : Shee is a comfort of Calamity, and in pro-
sperity a companion, a Physician in sicknesse, and a
Musician in helpe : her wayes are the walke toward
heauen , and her Guide is the Grace of the Almighty : She is her husbands Downe-bed, where his

heart

heart lyes at reft , and her childrens Glaffe in the notes of her Grace , her feruants honour in the keeping of her houfe , and her neighbours example in the notes of a good nature: She skorns Fortune, and loues Vertue , and out of thrift gathereth Charity : fhe is a Turtle in her loue , a Lambe in her meeke-neffe , a Saint in her heart , and an Angell in her foule. In fumme , fhee is a Iewell vnprizeable, and a ioy vnfpeakable , a comfort in Nature incompara-ble, and a Wife in the world vnmatchable.

An Vnquiet Woman.

AN Vnquiet Woman is the mifery of man, whofe demeanure is not to be defcribed, but in extremities : her voice is the skrieching of an Owle, her eye the poifon of a Cockatrice, her hand the clawe of a Crocadile, and her heart a Ca-binet of horrour : She is the griefe of Nature , the wound of Wit, the trouble of Reafon, and the ab-ufe of time : her pride is vnfupportable, her anger vnquenchable , her will vnfatiable , and her malice vnmatchable : She feares no colours, fhe cares for no counfaile, fhe fpares no perfons, nor refpects any time; her command is *Muft*, her Reafon *will*, her Refolution *Shall*, and her fatisfaction *So* : She looks at no lawe, and thinkes of no Lord, admits no com-maund, and keepes no good order : She is a croffe, but not of Chrift , and a word, but not of Grace , a creature, but not of wifedome, and a feruant, but not of God.. In fumme, fhe is the feede of trouble, the

37

fruit

fruit of trauaile, the taste of bitternesse, and the dige-
stion of death.

A good Wife.

38   A Good Wife is a world of wealth, where iust
cause of content makes a kingdome in conceit : She is the eye of warinesse, the tongue
of silence, the hand of labour, and the heart of loue:
a companion of kindnesse, a Mistris of Passion, an
exercise of Patience, and an example of experience :
She is the Kitchin Physician, the Chamber comfort,
the Halls care, and the Parlours Grace : She is the
Dairies neatnesse, the Brue-house wholsomnesse, the
Garners prouision, and the Gardens plantation : her
voice is musicke, her countenance meekenesse, her
minde vertuous, and her soule gracious : she is her
Husbands Iewell, her Childrens ioy, her Neighbors
loue, and her seruants honour; she is Pouerties prai-
er, and Charities praise, Religions loue, and Deuo-
tions zeale : she is a care of necessity, and a course of
Thrift, a booke of Huswifery, and a mirror of mode-
stie. In summe, she is Gods blessing, and Mans hap-
pinesse, Earths honour, and Heauens creature.

An Effeminate Foole.

39   AN Effeminate foole is the figure of a Baby; he
loues nothing but gay, to look in a Glasse, to
keepe among Wenches, and, to play with
trifles: to feed on sweet meats, and to be daunced in
Laps, to be imbraced in Armes, and to be kissed on
the

the Cheeke : To talke Idlely, to looke demurely, to
goe Nicely, and to Laugh continually : To be his
Miſtreſſe ſeruant, and her Mayds maſter, his Fathers
Loue, and his Mothers none-Child; to play on a
Fiddle, and ſing a Loue-ſong, to weare ſweet Gloues,
and looke on fine things : To make purpoſes, and
write Verſes, deuiſe Riddles, and tell lies : To fol-
low Plaies, and ſtudy Daunces, to heare Newes,
and buy trifles : To ſigh for Loue, and weepe for
kindneſſe, and mourne for company, and bee ſicke
for faſhion : To ride in a Coach, and gallop a Hackney, to watch all Night, and ſleepe out the Morning:
to lie on a bed, and take Tobacco, and to ſend his
Page of an idle meſſage to his Miſtreſſe : to go vp-
pon Gigges, to haue his Ruffes ſet in print, to picke
his Teeth, and play with a Puppet.   In ſumme, hee
is a man-Childe, and a Womans man, a gaze of
Folly, and Wiſedomes griefe.

A Paraſite.

A Pariſite is the Image of iniquity, who for the
gaine of droſſe, is deuoted to all villanie : He
is a kinde of Thiefe, in committing of Burgla-
rie, when hee breakes into houſes with his tongue,
and pickes pockets with his flatterie : his face is bra-
zed that he cannot bluſh, and his hands are limed to
catch holde what hee can light on : his tongue is a
Bell (but not of the Church, except it be the Diuels)
to call his Pariſh to his ſeruice : hee is ſometime a
Pander to carry meſſages of ill meetings, and per-
haps hath ſome Eloquence to perſwade ſweetneſſe

40

in finne : he is like a dogge at a doore, while the diuels dance in the chamber, or like a Spider in the
houfe top, that liues on the poifon belowe : hee is
the hate of honefty, and the abufe of beauty, the
fpoile of Youth, and the mifery of Age. In fumme,
he is a danger in a Court, a Cheater in a Citie, a Ie-
fter in the Countrey, and a Iacke-an-Apes in all.

A Bawde.

41

A Bawde is a kinde of Woman-Beaft, who hauing loft the honour of her Virginity in her
youth, meanes to goe to hell in her Age :
She is dangerous among young people, for feare of
the infection of the falling ficknefle, and not to teach
children to fpel, left fhe learne them too foone to put
together : fhee is partly a Surgeon, but moft for the
the allaying of fwellings in the lower parts, and hath
commonly a charme to coniure the Diuell into hell:
Shee grieues at nothing more, then at difability to
finne, and is neuer fo merry, as when fhe is perfwa-
ded to be young : fhe feares nothing more then the
Cart, and cares for nothing but eafe, and loues a
cup of Sacke and a pot of Ale, almoft as well as the
hope of her faluation : fhee is much fubiect to fore
eyes, and ill teeth, with fitting vp late, and feeding
on fweete things : fhe is a Goffip at a Childe-birth,
where, her mirth is a bawdy tale; and a Matrone in
an Hofpitall, to fee young wenches well fet to worke.
In fumme, fhee is the loathfomenefle of Nature, the
hate of Vertue, the fpoile of wealth, and the ruine of
Mayden-heads.

A Drun-

A Drunkard.

A Drunkard is a Nowne Adiectiue, for he cannot   42
stand alone by himselfe ; yet in his greateſt
weaknesse, a great trier of ſtrength, whether
health or ſickneſſe will haue the vpper hand in a ſurfet :
He is a ſpectacle of deformitie, and a ſhame of humanity, a viewe of ſinne, and a griefe of Nature : he is the
anoiance of Modeſty, and the trouble of Ciuility, the
ſpoile of wealth, and the ſpight of Reaſon : he is only
the Bruers Agent, and the Ale-houſe Benefactor, the
Beggers Companion, and the Conſtables trouble : he
is his Wifes woe, his Childrens ſorrow, his Neighbours ſcoffe, and his owne ſhame. In ſumme, hee is a
Tubbe of ſwill, a Spirit of ſleepe, a picture of a Beaſt,
and a Monſter of a man.

A Coward.

A Coward is the childe of feare, hee was begotten in colde bloud, when Nature had much a-   43
doe to make vp a Creature like a man : his life
is a kinde of ſickneſſe, which breeds a kinde of palſey in
the ioynts, and his death the terror of his conſcience,
with the extreme weakeneſſe of his faith : hee loues
Peace as his life, for he feares a ſword in his ſoule : if
he cut his finger, hee looketh preſently for the ſigne,
and if his head ake, he is ready to make his will : a re-
port of a cannon ſtrikes him flat on his face, and a clap
of thunder makes him a ſtrange *Metamorphoſis*: rather
then he will fight, he will be beaten, and if his legges
F   will

will helpe him, he will put his armes to no trouble : he makes loue commonly with his purse , and brags most of his Mayden-head,he will not marry but into a quiet family, and not too faire a wife,to auoide quarrels : if his wife frowne vpon him, he sighes , and if shee giue him an vnkinde word , he weepes : hee loues not the hornes of a Bull , nor the pawes of a Beare : and if a dogge barke, he will not come neere the house : if hee be rich,he is afraide of Theeues, and if he be poore he will be slaue to a Begger. In summe, hee is the shame of man-hood , the disgrace of Nature , the skorne of Reason, and the hate of honour.

An honest Poore man.

44   AN honest Poore man is the proofe of miserie, where patience is put to the trial of her strength to endure griefe without passion , in staruing with concealed necessity, or standing in the aduentures of Charitie : if he be married, Want rings in his eares, and woe watreth his eyes : if single, he droopeth with the shame of Beggery, or dyes with the passion of pe- nurie : of the Rich, he is shunned like infection , and of the poore learnes but a heart-breaking profession : his bed is the earth, and the heauen is his Canapy, the Sunne is his Summers comfort, and the Moone is his Winter candle : his sighes are the notes of his musick, and his Song is like the Swanne before her death : his study, his patience, and his exercise prayer ; his dyet, the herbes of the earth, and his drinke,the water of the Riuer: his trauell is the walke of the woful,and his horse *Bayard* of ten-toes : his apparell but the clothing of na-
                                         kednesse

kedneſſe, and his wealth but the hope of heauen : He is a ſtranger in the world, for no man craues his acquaintance, & his funerall is without Ceremony, when there is no mourning for the miſſe of him : yet may he be in the ſtate of Election, and in the life of loue, and more rich in Grace, then the greateſt of the World. In ſum, he is the griefe of Nature , the ſorrow of Reaſon, the pittie of wiſedome, and the charge of Charity.

A Iuſt man.

A Iuſt man is the Child of Truth, begotten by vertue and kindneſſe , when Nature in the temper of the ſpirit, made euen the ballance of Indifferency : his eye is cleere from blindneſſe, and his hand from Bribery , his will from wilfulneſſe, and his heart from wickedneſſe : his word and deed are all one, his life ſhewes the nature of his loue, his care is the charge of his Conſcience, and his comfort, the aſſurance of his Saluation : In the Seat of Iuſtice , he is the grace of the Lawe, and in the iudgement of Right , the honour of Reaſon : he feares not the power of Authority to equall Iuſtice with Mercie, and ioyes but in the iudgement of Grace, to ſee the execution of Iuſtice : his Iudgement is worthy of honour, and his Wiſedome is gracious in Truth : his Honour is famous in Vertue, and his Vertue is precious in Example. In ſumme, he is a ſpirit of Vnderſtanding, a braine of Knowledge , a heart of Wiſedome, and a Soule of Bleſſedneſſe.

45

A Repentant Sinner.

46

A Repentant Sinner is the Child of Grace, who being borne for the seruice of God, makes no reckoning of the mastershippe of the world, yet, doth he glorifie God in the beholding of his creatures, and in giuing praise to his holy Name, in the admiration of his Work-manship: He is much of the nature of an Angell, who being sent into the world but to do the will of his Master, is euer longing to bee at home with his fellowes : He desires nothing but that is necessary, and delighteth in nothing that is transitory, but contemplates more then hee can conceiue, and meditates onely vpon the Word of the Almighty; his Senses are the tyrers of his Spirit, while, in the course of nature, his Soule can find no rest: He shakes off the ragges of Sinne, and is cloathed with the Robe of Vertue: he puts off *Adam*, and puts on Christ : His heart is the Anuile of Truth, where the braine of his Wisedome beates the thoughts of his Minde, till they be fit for the seruice of his Maker : His labour is the trauaile of Loue, by the rule of Grace to find the high-way to Heauen : His feare is greater then his Loue of the World, and his Loue is greater then his feare of God. In summe, he is in the Election of Loue, in the booke of Life, an Angell incarnate, and a blessed Creature.

A Reprobate.

A Reprobate is the Childe of finne, who being borne for the feruice of the Deuill, cares not what villany he does in the world : His wit is alwaies in a maze, for his courfes are euer out of order, and while his will ftands for his wifedome, the beft that fals out of him, is a Foole : Hee betrayes the truft of the fimple, and fucks out the blood of the Innocent. His breath is the fume of Blafphemy, and his Tongue the fire-brand of Hell : His defires are the deftruction of the Vertuous, and his delights are the Traps to damnation : Hee bathes in the bloud of Murther, and fups vp the broth of Iniquity : He frighteth the Eyes of the Godly, & difturbeth the hearts of the Religious: he marreth the wits of the Wife, and is hatefull to the Soules of the Gracious. In fumme, he is an inhumane Creature, a fearefull Companion, a man-Monfter, and a Diuell incarnate.

47

An Old man.

AN Old man is the declaration of Time, in the defect of nature, and the imperfection of fenfe in the vfe of Reafon : He is in the obferuation of Time, a Kalender of experience, but in the power of Action, he is a blanke among Lots : He is the fubiect of weakeneffe, the Agent of fickneffe, the difpleafure of life, and the forerunner of death : Hee is twife a Child, and halfe a man, a liuing Picture, and a dying Creature : he is a blowne Bladder, that is onely ftuffed

48

with

with winde, and a withered Tree , that hath loft the
fappe of the Roote: or an old Lute with ftrings all bro-
ken, or a ruined Caftle that is ready to fall : Hee is the
eye-fore of Youth, and the ieft of Loue, and in the ful-
neffe of Infirmitie, the Mirror of Mifery. Yet, in the
honour of Wifedome, he may be Gracious in Graui-
ty, and in the gouernment of Iuftice, deferue the Honour of Reuerence: Yea, his Words may be notes for
the vfe of Reafon, and his Actions examples for the
imitation of difcretion. In fumme, in whatfoeuer e-
ftate, he is but as the fnuffe of a Candle, that pinke it
neuer fo long, it will out at laft.

A Young man.

49   A Young man is the Spring of Time, when Nature in her Pride fhewes her Beauty to the
World: He is the delight of the Eye, and the
ftudy of the minde, the labour of inftruction, and the
Pupil of Reafon:His Wit is in making or marring,his
Wealth in gaining or lofing, his Honour in aduan-
cing or declining, and his Life in abridging or increa-
fing : He is a Bloome, that either is blafted in the Bud,
or growes to a good fruit,or a Bird that dies in the neft,
or liues to make vfe of her wings : Hee is a Colt that
muft haue a Bridle , ere hee bee well managed, and a
Faulcon that muft be well man'd, or hee will neuer be
reclaimde : Hee is the Darling of Nature, and the
charge of Reafon, the exercife of Patience, and the
hope of Charity : His exercife is either Study or
Action, and his ftudy either Knowledge or Pleafure :
His difpofition giues a great note of his generation,

and

and yet, his breeding may eyther better or worſe him, though to wiſh a Black-Moore white, bee the loſſe of labour, and what is bred in the bone, will neuer out of the fleſh. In ſumme, till experience haue ſeaſoned his Vnderſtanding, hee is rather a Childe then a man, a prey of flattery, or a praiſe of prouidence, in the way of Grace, to proue a Saint, or in the way of ſinne, to grow a Deuill.

A Holy man.

A Holy man is the chiefeſt Creature in the worke-manſhip of the World : He is the higheſt in the Election of Loue, and the neereſt to the I-mage of the humane Nature of his Maker : Hee is ſerued of all the creatures in the Earth, and created but for the ſeruice of his Creator : Hee is capable of the courſe of Nature, and by the rule of Obſeruati-on, finds the Art of Reaſon; his ſenſes are but ſer-uants to his Spirit, which is guided by a power aboue himſelfe : his Time is onely knowne to the Eye of the Almighty, and what hee is in his moſt greatneſſe, is as nothing, but in his Mercy : He makes Law by the direction of life, and liues but in the mercy of Loue: he treads vpõ the face of the Earth, til in the ſame ſubſtãce he be trod vpon, though his Soule that gaue life to his ſenſes, liue in Heauen, till the reſurrection of his fleſh : Hee hath an Eye to looke vpward to-wards Grace, while Labour is onely the puniſh-ment of ſinne: his Faith is the hand of his Soule, which layeth hold on the promiſe of Mercy : his Patience, the Tenure of the poſſeſſion of his Soule,

　　　　　　　　　　　　　　　　　　　his

his Charity, the rule of his life, and his hope, the An-
chor of his Saluation : His study is the state of Obedience, and his exercise the continuance of Prayer; his
life but a passage to a better, and his death, the rest
of his labours : His heart is a watch to his Eye,
his wit, a doore to his Mouth, his Soule, a guard to his
Spirit, and his Limmes, but labourers for his Body.
In summe, hee is rauisht with Diuine Loue,
hatefull to the nature of Sinne, troubled with
the Vanities of the World, and longing
. for his Ioy but in Hea-
uen.

F I N I S,